Bruce McMillan

APPLES

How They Grow

Photographs by Bruce McMillan

Houghton Mifflin Company Boston 1979

For Bob and Al

This book is the culmination of two years' work. One year was spent in the orchard learning and sketching photographically. This was followed by a second year in which I took the final photographs, knowing by now what was important in the apple's development and what changes to expect.

The three apple varieties photographed at McDougal's Orchard, Springvale, Maine were:
McIntosh, the old standby first discovered by John McIntosh in 1810 at Ontario, Canada.
Cortland, a cross between the McIntosh and Ben Davis varieties developed in 1915 at the New York Experimental Station.
Jerseymac, a McIntosh type that ripens early, developed at the New Jersey Experimental Station from mixed parentage.

Library of Congress Cataloging in Publication Data

McMillan, Bruce.
  Apples, how they grow.

  SUMMARY: Describes how apples grow, from dormant bud to ripe fruit.
  1. Apple—Juvenile literature. [1. Apple] I. Title.
SB363.M15   583'.372   78-27147
ISBN 0-395-27806-6

H   10 9 8 7 6 5 4 3 2 1

Acknowledgments

If there was anything I needed — a helping hand, a ride on the snowmobile to get through the snow to the back orchard, a phone call to keep me posted on the apple's stage of growth, anything at all — two people were always there: Bob McDougal, owner and operator of McDougal's Orchards, Twin Ridge Corporation, Springvale, Maine; and orchardist Al Reay, Bob's "right hand." They always made it even more of a pleasure to photograph in the apple orchard.

Two fruit scientists were helpful with their pomological advice: noted plant breeder Dr. Elwyn Meader, Rochester, New Hampshire; and Maine Extension Fruit Specialist, Dr. Warren Stiles, Highmoor Farm, Monmouth, Maine.

And of course, for eating all those juicy red apples, Wylie Herzberg and his mother Sue, and Heather Dowdell and her mother Michelle.

Cold winter is a time of rest for the apple tree.
But everything is there, ready to grow apples.

The tips of some of the branches are the fruiting spurs, and the large plump buds on these spurs are the flower buds, formed the summer before. Inside each bud are all the tiny flowering parts, protected by the bud scales wrapped around them. Under the right conditions, it is these flower buds that will form the apples.

The flower (or fruit) buds and their leaves are the first to swell and burst open.

When spring comes with its longer, warm days and the sap inside the trees starts to flow, the winter rest is over and dormancy is broken. Silver tips push aside the bud scales and emerge. Later, the shoot buds will open, growing new branches and leaves. But without the necessary cold of winter the tree could not start the new year's growth.

When the cluster of leaves is about half an inch long, the outer layer begins to spread out. At the center of the cluster something other than leaves is growing.

The buds have continued to grow and swell until green tips, the first sign of leaves, emerge, growing in a tight green bunch.

As the outer layer of leaves spreads,
the blossom buds which were hidden
inside emerge above them.

*Seen from afar, small specks of green leaves
and blossom clusters dot the apple trees.*

The center blossom bud is surrounded by five more buds, forming a tight cluster.

Each bud is enclosed by five green sepals. As the blossom buds grow they force this part of the flower back, and the green of the sepals is replaced by the emerging scarlet red petals.

With the green leaves at the base of the bud cluster making the necessary food, the buds grow and spread out.

The flower petals, at first red, turn pink as they continue to grow.

The central — or king — blossom is the first one to spread its five flower petals and bloom.

As each flower opens, the petals keep getting lighter in color until, when fully in bloom, they look almost white.

At the center of each blossom are the male and female parts of the flower.

On the stamens, which are the male flower organs, there are twenty filaments located at the base of the flower petals. At their tips pollen is produced. These surround the female organ, the pistil, whose five sticky tips catch the powdery pollen. Pollination occurs when the pollen is deposited on the sticky end of the pistil.

To produce apples the flowers in most varieties must be cross-pollinated; bees deposit the pollen from the flower of one apple variety onto the flower of another.

Bees carry the pollen of different apple varieties from tree to tree, cross-pollinating the blossoms.

In the course of a sunny day, one honeybee may make a dozen trips from the hive and visit thousands of blossoms. Having used up their winter supply of honey, the bees gather the liquid nectar of the flower blossoms to make more honey and collect pollen to feed their brood. Some of the pollen adheres to their hairy bodies and rubs off on the sticky tips of the pistils. When this happens, and if the pollen is from different varieties of apple blossoms, cross-pollination is completed.

At the base of the blossom is a small swelling of the green stem. This is the ovary, which will grow into the apple once it has been fertilized.

The male pollen grain grows inside the pistil down to the ovule at the center of the swelling, and fertilizes it. Usually there are ten ovules inside the ovary which may grow into apple seeds.
With the branches of each tree speckled with blossoms, the entire tree is a mass of white. But that will not last long.

The king blossom, since it was first to bloom,
is the first to lose its white petals.

*Petal fall changes the appearance of the tree
as the white of the fallen petals is replaced by
the green of the growing leaves. Soon after
petal fall is complete, those blossoms that
were not pollinated wither and drop off. If
they were pollinated but did not get fertilized,
they will fall off the tree a few days later.*

As the rest of the flower parts wither, the swelling on the stem grows.

The apple tree starts to show signs of new growth. New branches shoot out producing more leaves. The once-white blossom-covered trees are now outlined in green.

The swelling continues to grow and begins to take a rounder shape.

The largest apple of the cluster will grow from what was once the king blossom. The others will be relatively small in size.

The tiny hairlike growths, which give it a fuzzy appearance when it is small, are changed by the growing apple. Eventually the skin will take on a smooth sheen.

If all the apples in the cluster continue to grow they will not be as large as they could potentially be. The food available from the apple tree would not be enough to feed them all. At the end of spring some of the apples will fall off naturally. This is known as June drop.

It takes about forty leaves to make enough food for one apple to grow to its full size.

By early summer the trees are dense with green foliage, each leaf a miniature food factory. The leaves take in carbon dioxide gas from the air around them, water with mineral nutrients which the roots and trunk carry up from the soil, and sunlight. In the presence of chlorophyll, which gives the leaves their green color, they make food in the form of sugars for the tree as well as for the growing apples. This process is called photosynthesis, and the produced sugars, or carbohydrates, are transported throughout the tree by the tissues just beneath the bark.

Now, with only one or two apples left in each cluster to use the sugars produced by the leaves, the apples can continue to their full growth.

At the base of the stem, another short shoot may be developing on the fruiting spur. This is the start of next year's apples, the developing bud that will winter over and blossom next spring.

With the apple blossom now withered away,
the remaining sepals are dwarfed
by the growing apple.

*As the summer progresses the dense green
foliage is dotted with round green apples.
The branches of the tree hang low under the
increasing weight of the growing apples.
Sometimes, if the branches are weak, they
will break off.*

By the end of summer the green apple is almost full size.

The rains and sunlight, along with nutrients from the soil, have kept everything growing. In addition to the easily seen changes taking place above ground, much has been happening underground as well. The tree's roots have been growing and spreading, keeping a balance with its growth above. They spread underground as far as or even beyond the drip line, an invisible circle on the ground around the tree where raindrops fall from the outermost leaves.

In the clear crisp days of fall the last stage of the apple's growth takes place. It ripens.

The complex sugars, or carbohydrates, break down into simple sugars, transforming the hard, tart green apple into a soft, sweet-tasting one. The full-sized green apples usually turn red, although some varieties turn yellow in ripening, while others stay green. The apples that have grown at the outer edges of the tree, thus getting the full sunlight, will be larger and redder than those growing deep inside the foliage.

A ripe, red apple on the tree means it is ready for picking.

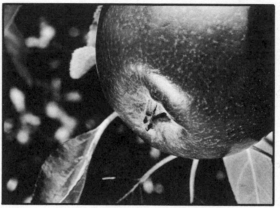

All that remains at the flower end of the apple are the withered sepals. The stem end is attached to the fruiting spur where next year's fruit buds are already formed. When picked, the apple should break at a weakened point where the stem joins the fruiting spur. Nothing other than the apple and its stem should come off. A careless picker could tear off next year's crop by pulling off leaves and the fruiting spur along with the apple.

Although some apple varieties are softer and bruise more easily than others, all apples can be damaged if not handled carefully when they are picked.

The best way to make sure the apples are ripe
is to take a good, juicy bite.

Glossary

Bloom The flower or blossom of the apple tree.

Carbohydrates Chemical compounds, such as sugars and starches, which are composed of carbon, hydrogen, and oxygen and which are produced by plants.

Chlorophyll Green pigments found in green plants. These are necessary for photosynthesis.

Cross-pollinate To pollinate a flower of one variety with pollen from another variety.

Dormant An inactive or resting condition in which plant processes are slowed down or suspended.

Fertilization The process of reproduction, where the male pollen combines with the female ovule.

Fruiting spur A short, stunted branch of a tree, on which the fruit will grow.

June drop The natural fall of partially developed apple fruits.

King blossom The center blossom of the flower cluster.

Nectar A sweet liquid secreted by flowers and gathered by bees for making honey.

Ovule The small female part at the base of the flower which, when fertilized, becomes the apple seed.

Petals The brightly colored parts of the flower blossom, in the apple starting as scarlet red, becoming pink, then almost white.

Photosynthesis The process by which chlorophyll-containing cells convert sunlight, carbon dioxide gas, and water into carbohydrates and oxygen.

Pistil The female organ of the flower blossom.

Pollen The fine powderlike material produced by the male organs of the flower blossom. This is the male component of fertilization.

Pollinate To carry or transfer pollen from the male organ of the flower, where it is produced, to the female organ.

Sepal One of the five green parts of the flower, attached at its base, and covering the newly formed flowers. The sepals wither as the apple grows.

Stamen The pollen-producing male reproductive organ of the flower.